Raffi Songs to Read®

This Little Light of Mine

Alfred A. Knopf • New York

Adapted by
Raffi

Illustrated by
Stacey Schuett

For Clare and Ian, little lights both.
—S.S.

THIS IS A BORZOI BOOK PUBLISHED BY ALFRED A. KNOPF
Text copyright © 1982 by Homeland Publishing (SOCAN)
Illustrations copyright © 2004 by Stacey Schuett
Front cover photograph © Colin Goldie, GM Studios
Back cover photograph © 2004 by Carrie Nuttall
All rights reserved under International and Pan-American Copyright Conventions. Published
in the United States of America by Alfred A. Knopf, an imprint of Random House Children's
Books, a division of Random House, Inc., New York, and simultaneously in Canada by
Random House of Canada Limited, Toronto. Distributed by Random House, Inc., New York.

RAFFI SONGS TO READ and SONGS TO READ are registered trademarks of Troubadour Learning,
a division of Troubadour Records, Ltd.

KNOPF, BORZOI BOOKS, and the colophon are registered trademarks of Random House, Inc.

www.randomhouse.com/kids

Library of Congress Cataloging-in-Publication Data is available upon request.

ISBN 0-375-82871-0 (trade)
ISBN 0-375-92871-5 (lib. bdg.)

Printed in the United States of America
June 2004
10 9 8 7 6 5 4 3 2 1
First Edition

This little light of mine,
I'm gonna let it shine.

This little light of mine,
I'm gonna let it shine.

This little light of mine,
I'm gonna let it shine.
Let it shine, let it shine,
Let it shine.

I'm gonna take this light around the world
And I'm gonna let it shine.

I'm gonna take this light around the world
And I'm gonna let it shine.

I'm gonna take this light around the world
And I'm gonna let it shine.

Let it shine, let it shine,
Let it shine.

This little light of mine,
I'm gonna let it shine.

This little light of mine,

I'm gonna let it shine.

This little light of mine,

I'm gonna let it shine.

Let it shine, let it shine,
Let it shine.

I won't let anyone blow it out,
I'm gonna let it shine.
I won't let anyone blow it out,

I'm gonna let it shine.
I won't let anyone blow it out,
I'm gonna let it shine.

This little light of mine,
I'm gonna let it shine.

This little light of mine,

I'm gonna let it shine.

This little light of mine,
I'm gonna let it shine.

Let it shine, let it shine,
Let it shine.

Every day, every day,
I'm gonna let my little light shine.

This Little Light of Mine

traditional; adapted by Raffi

Lyrics below the staff:

This lit-tle light of mine, I'm gon-na let it shine. This lit-tle light of mine, I'm gon-na let it shine. This lit-tle light of mine, I'm gon-na let it shine. Let it shine, let it shine, let it shine.

I'm gonna take this light around the world
And I'm gonna let it shine.
I'm gonna take this light around the world
And I'm gonna let it shine.
I'm gonna take this light around the world
And I'm gonna let it shine.
Let it shine, let it shine,
Let it shine.

This little light of mine,
I'm gonna let it shine.
This little light of mine,
I'm gonna let it shine.
This little light of mine,
I'm gonna let it shine.
Let it shine, let it shine,
Let it shine.

I won't let anyone blow it out,
I'm gonna let it shine.
I won't let anyone blow it out,
I'm gonna let it shine.
I won't let anyone blow it out,
I'm gonna let it shine.

This little light of mine,
I'm gonna let it shine.
This little light of mine,
I'm gonna let it shine.
This little light of mine,
I'm gonna let it shine.
Let it shine, let it shine,
Let it shine.

Every day, every day,
I'm gonna let my little light
shine.